A BOY
JUST
FOR ME

A BOY JUST FOR ME

Ed Young

Story by

Dorothea P. Seeber

PUFFIN BOOKS

Patricia Lee Gauch, editor

PUFFIN BOOKS
Published by the Penguin Group
Penguin Putnam Books for Young Readers,
345 Hudson Street, New York, New York 10014, U.S.A.
Penguin Books Ltd, 27 Wrights Lane, London W8 5TZ, England
Penguin Books Australia Ltd, Ringwood, Victoria, Australia
Penguin Books Canada Ltd, 10 Alcorn Avenue, Toronto, Ontario, Canada M4V 3B2
Penguin Books (N.Z.) Ltd, 182-190 Wairau Road, Auckland 10, New Zealand

Penguin Books Ltd, Registered Offices: Harmondsworth, Middlesex, England

First published in the United States of America by Philomel Books,
a division of Penguin Putnam Books for Young Readers, 2000
Published by Puffin Books, a division of Penguin Putnam Books for Young Readers, 2002

1 3 5 7 9 10 8 6 4 2

THE LIBRARY OF CONGRESS HAS CATALOGED THE PHILOMEL EDITION AS FOLLOWS:
Seeber, Dorothea P.
A pup just for me ; A boy just for me / by Dorothea P. Seeber ; illustrations by Ed Young
p.   cm.
Summary: A rhyming story about a boy who is offered every kind of pet except the puppy
he wants. When the book is turned over, the story is told from the dog's point of view.
1. Upside-down books—Specimens. [1. Pets—Fiction. 2. Dogs—Fiction. 3. Stories in Rhyme. 4. Upside-down books.]
I. Young, Ed, ill. II. Title. III. Title: Pup just for me ; A boy just for me. IV. Title: Boy just for me.
PZ8.3.S45Pu 2000 [E]—dc21 98-45702 CIP AC
ISBN: 0-399-23403-9 (hc)

This edition ISBN 0-698-11927-4

Printed in Hong Kong

Once there was a pup
who wanted a boy.
He whined for him
begged for him
barked for him.

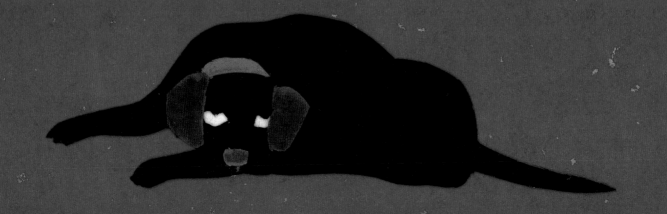

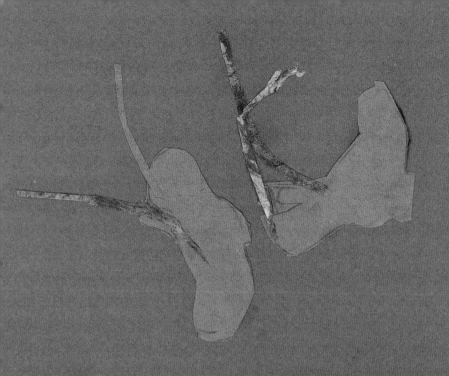

But the first owner Jet had was a
Mister Brumblepaster
who beat him and kicked him
to show he was master.

So Jet ran away
in search of a boy
who would stroke his black silky ears
and cuddle away his haunted fears.

Joanna Jellibee took Jet to her home.
She gave him some milk and she gave him a bone,
but she never had any time for play,
and Jet was tied in the yard each day.

So Jet ran away
in search of a boy
who wanted to play
the whole live-long day.

But Jet's next home was
with three small tots.
They dressed him in denim
with his hair tied in knots;
they wheeled him up,
they wheeled him down.
In the dollbaby's carriage
he looked like a clown.

So Jet ran away to look for a boy
who would run in the woods with him
or throw him a toy
that Jet could bring back to him
with wriggling joy.

The station agent
was a lonely man.
He sat in the ticket office
at Prann
with only the hail
of the Night Train's wail.
In the night Jet came and jumped the track!
The lonely man tried to whistle him back,

but—

Jet ran away
in search of a boy
who would give him a bed
for his silky black head.

When Miss Lydia B. Twitty (who lived in the city
and kept twenty-two cats and one little kitty)
saw Jet trotting by, she gave a quick cry,
"Come be a guard for the cats in my yard!"

Jet flew in a huff from his tail to his scruff.
He felt so insulted he quick catapulted
to the center of town
to where Main crosses Brown.

"Look here, Black Beauty," a man said then,
"I see that you're tramping these streets again.
You're tired and you're thin and
    your footpads are sore.
Come stay in our Home
and wander no
more."

Jet was right glad to sink down and rest
in his big strawlined box like a feathered nest.
But after he'd eaten and slept in that room
all the dogs broke out in a high barking boom.

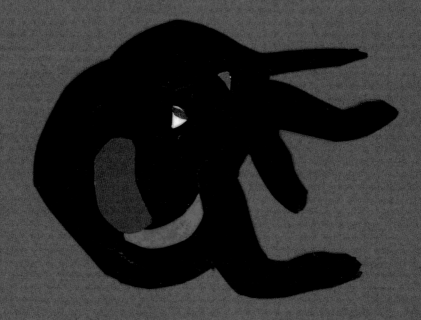

Something was moving the length of the hall,
something in blue jeans and not very tall.
Jet sniffed the air, then wriggled his nose.

His tail, like a flag, ever higher rose.
Deep down in his throat Jet barked for joy:
He'd found him! He'd found him!

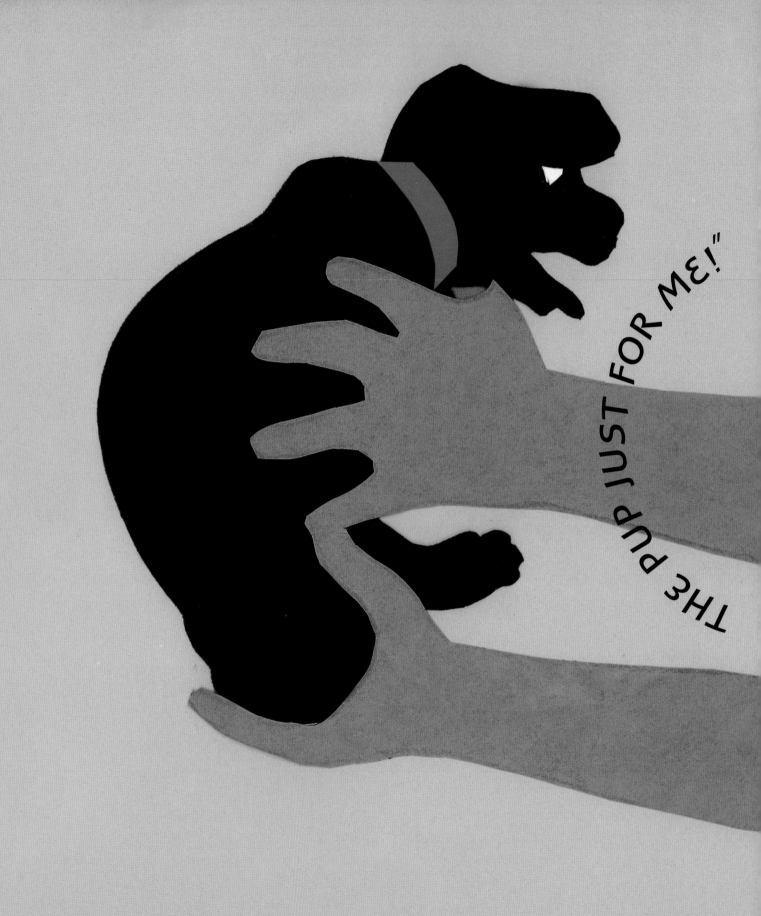

THE PUP JUST FOR ME!"

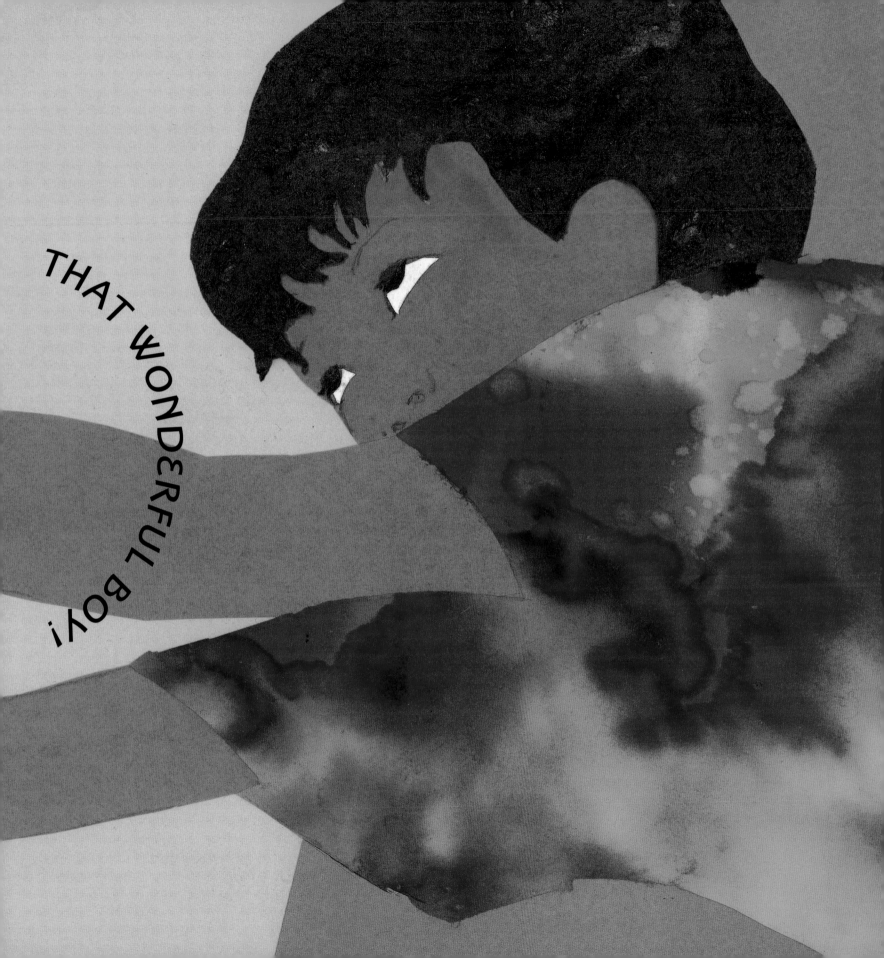

THAT WONDERFUL BOY!

He looked each one down and he looked each one up.
When he came upon ONE, he cried out in glee,
"I found him, I found him,

They took Rod to the room full of puppies in boxes.
Some were small, some big, some looked like young foxes.
Roddy looked deep in the eyes of each pup.

"A puppy," he gasped,
"is the one thing I need.
Please give me a pup
I can train and can feed.
We'll run through the woods
in the sun and the wet,
if only you'll give me
a pup for a pet."

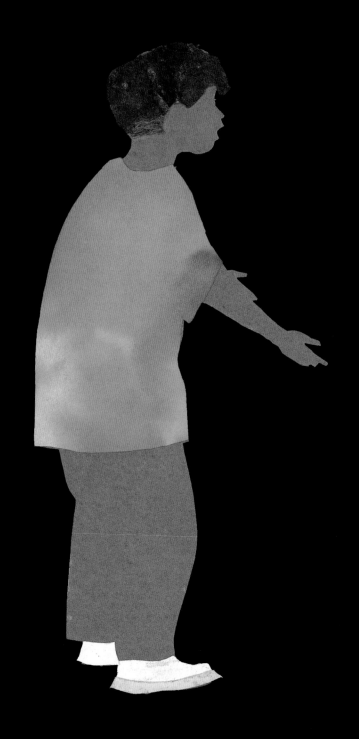

Poor Roddy flew out of his house to the lane.

He raced to the village, to the corner of Main.

He turned left at Main Street and dashed to the Home

where they care for stray animals that always must roam.

"But rabbits can't play hide 'n seek," cried Roddy.
"They always have babies and wriggle their noses
and spend their time in afternoon dozes.
The pet that I want is a
puppy!"

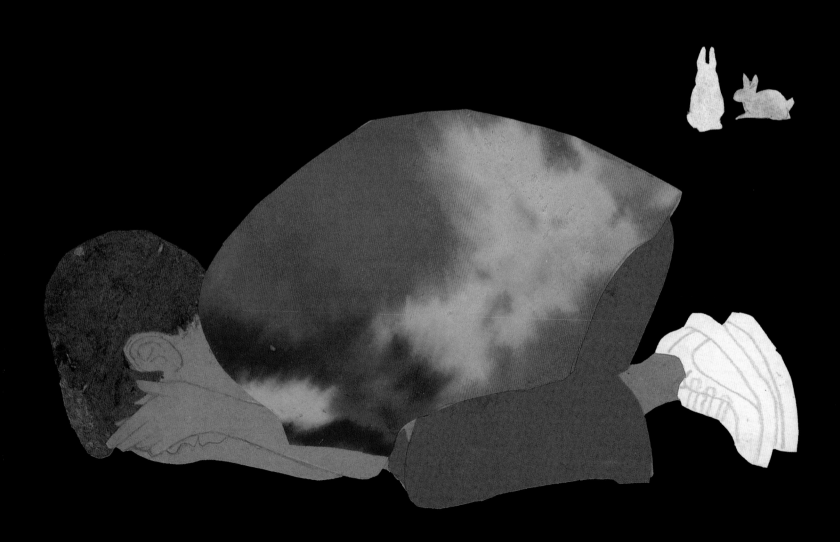

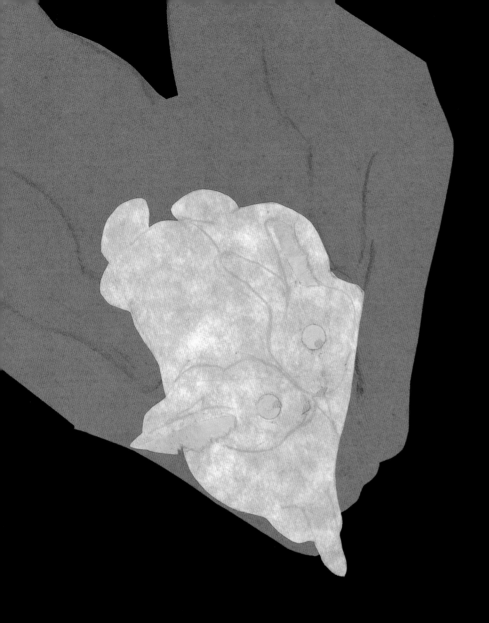

Big Uncle Hal called Rod on the phone.
He had wonderful news—you could tell by his tone.
"Our rabbits have lots of new babies again!
Please, Roddy, come over and take two of them."

"But goldfish can't sleep on my bed," cried Roddy.
"They're slimy and slippy, cold and all drippy.
The pet that I want is a
puppy!"

"Goldfish are nice,"
said plump Polly Price.
"They gleam and they glimmer,
they shine and they shimmer.
I'll give some to Roddy."

"But canaries can't fetch," cried Roddy.
"They just swing on their feet
and keep saying 'tweet tweet.'
The pet that I want is a
puppy!"

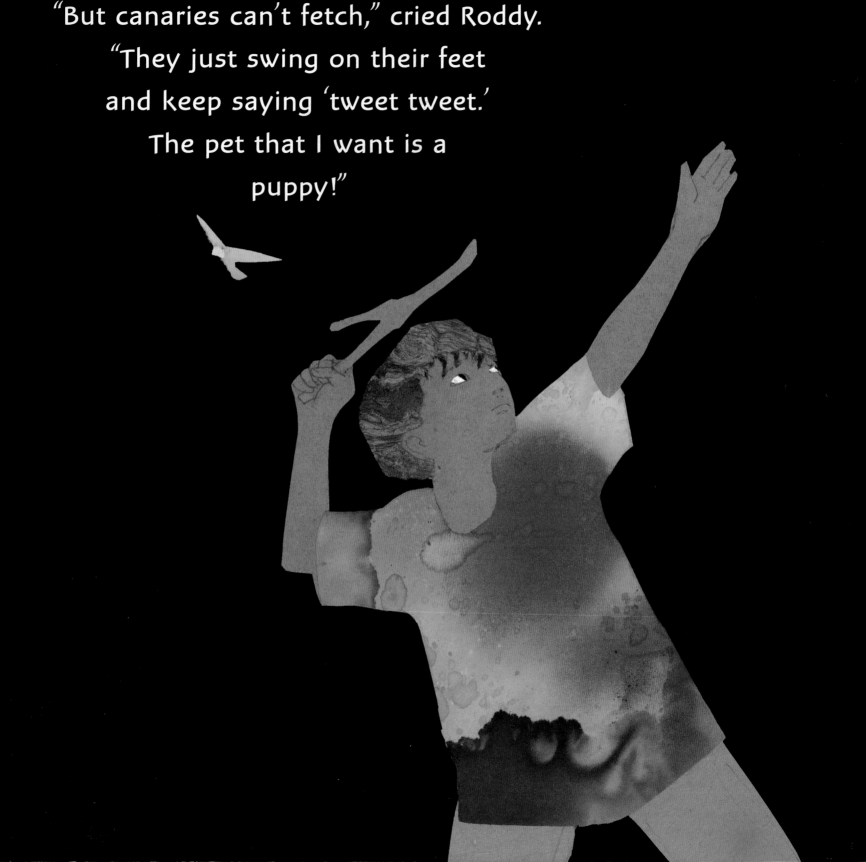

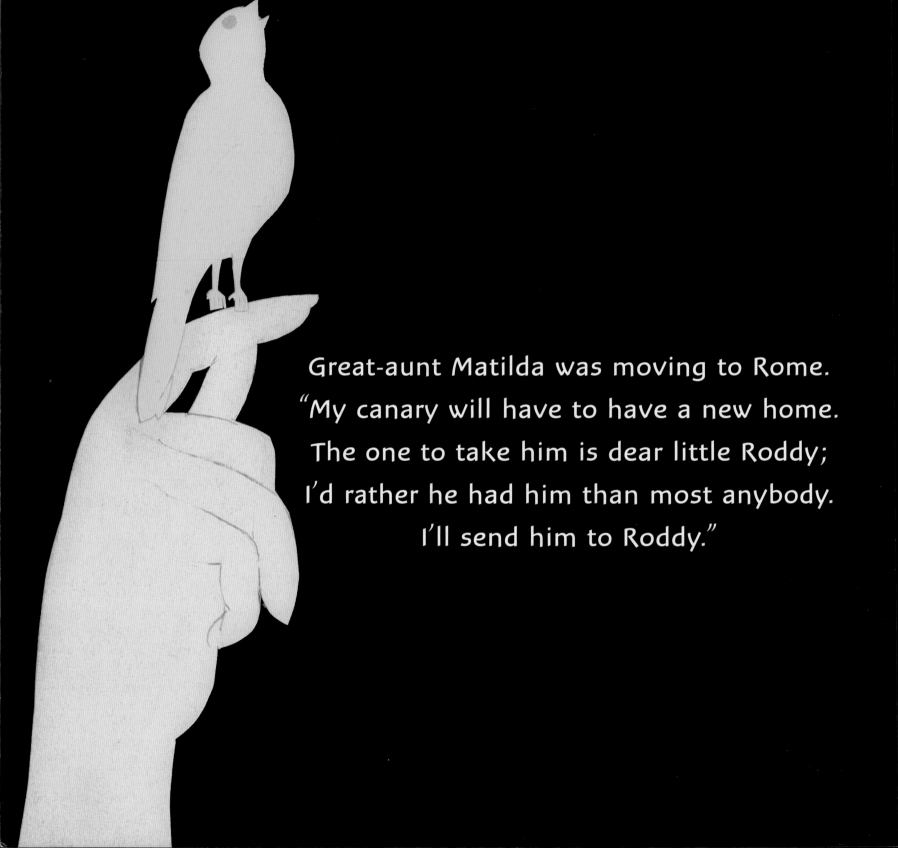

Great-aunt Matilda was moving to Rome.
"My canary will have to have a new home.
The one to take him is dear little Roddy;
I'd rather he had him than most anybody.
I'll send him to Roddy."

"But turtles can't run," cried Roddy.
"They stand and they crawl and that's about all.
The pet that I want is a
puppy!"

Now Dad took a hand:
"A turtle I had
when I was a lad.
It takes up no space
and moves at slow pace.
I'll get Rod a turtle."

"But cats are no good," cried Roddy.
"When you want to play,
they just run away.
The pet that I want is a
puppy!"

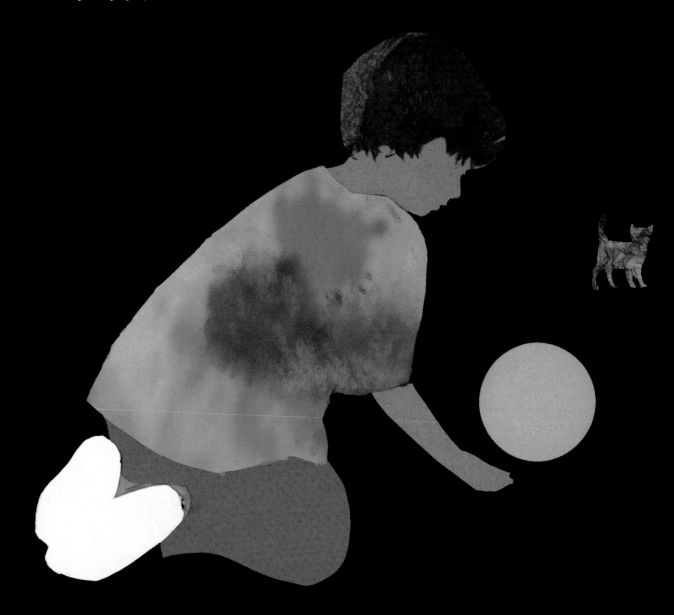

Mother said,
"Rod needs a pet.
I'll get him a kitty.
It's cute and it's cuddly,
playful and pretty.
I'll get him a kitty."

Once there was a boy named Roddy
who wanted a pup.
He asked for it,
begged for it,
prayed for it.

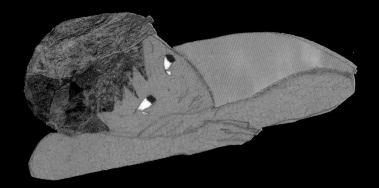

For Betty Perkins Aldrich,
a lifetime friend who has never failed
—D. S.

To the matchmakers, Robert and Janetta
—E. Y.

A PUP JUST FOR ME

Ed Young

Story by

Dorothea P. Seeber

PUFFIN BOOKS

A PUP
JUST
FOR ME